TEACAN - age 5

To: Tennessee Don -

Renée Wendinger

# Charlie's Chalk Stick

Written by Renée Wendinger

Illustrated by Sharon Grey

*Charlie's Chalk Stick*
Written by Renée Wendinger
Illustrated by Sharon Grey

Published by Legendary Publications, Minnesota
ISBN: 9780991360338
Library of Congress Control Number: 2015918076
First Edition

## Dedication:

An immense thank you to my parents, Charles and Sophia Hillesheim, and the neighborhood of Second and Elm Streets, for motivating this story by way of empathic assistance offered to hobos of a bygone era.

To New York orphan train rider, Edward Miller, for persevering through hardships as a hobo to become a selfless man and outstanding citizen.

And to my grandchildren….
Jaydon, Lily, Alison, Landon, Karly, and Kenlee.
♥

EVERY STOP I MAKE,
I'LL MAKE A NEW FRIEND,
CAN'T STAY FOR LONG,
JUST TURN AROUND,
AND I'M GONE AGAIN.

HOBO CHARLIE

One hot summer's day a man wearing a coat full of holes and a dusty hat jumped off the two o'clock train when it rumbled into town. This was not an uncommon sight in those days. The Great Depression had taken away people's jobs and homes, and many of them were now riding the rails, looking for work and a better future.

Sometime ago Charlie had worked in a bank, but after losing his job he had left his hometown and was now a hobo, hopping from boxcar to boxcar hoping to find work somewhere so that he could buy food. What he really wanted was a steady job, but there were very few of these to be had.

That afternoon, nearby his home, Terry, a curious little boy, was playing his favorite spy game near the railroad tracks. He was having fun looking for clues with his magnifying glass when he saw a hobo getting off the train. Terry decided to follow the man at a distance. After all, that is what Dick Tracy would do if he saw someone suspicious come into town.

Charlie knew that there had to be a hobo village near the tracks and so he went to look for it. He was tired and hungry and hoped that he would be able to get something to eat at the camp, and find shelter for the night. It would be good to sit around a campfire with other hobos, sharing stories and bowls of Mulligan stew.

Soon Charlie found the hobo village. It was empty. Cold ashes in the fire pits told Charlie that the other hobos had left or had been forced to move on.

Terry hid himself from view behind one of the shacks, sneaking quick looks at the hobo. Terry was watching when a thin and dirty dog limped out from one of the shacks and headed towards the hobo.

"Hey there pup," Charlie said in a soft voice. He stooped down to pet the dog gently. "Looks like you hurt your leg," he added as he carefully looked at the wound. The dog whined, but looked trustingly at Charlie.

11

Charlie opened one of the bundles that was attached to the end of a long stick that he carried. He took out a piece of cloth and a tin dish. He filled the container with water from a rain barrel that stood next to one of the shacks. Carefully, Charlie cleaned the dog's wound, and then bandaged the leg with his last handkerchief. Next, he gave the dog his last bit of food; a stale piece of bread.

Just then Terry heard his mother calling his name. Carefully he moved away from the place where he had been hiding and then ran home. After checking in with his mother, Terry went to find out what the other kids in his neighborhood were doing. He found them setting up a lemonade stand in front of Sophie's house.

Eagerly, Terry told the kids about the new hobo who had come to town. He began to tell them about how the hobo had helped an injured dog, but was interrupted by Max.

"We don't like hobos coming to our town," Max said.

Jenny, Sophie's friend who was a walking dictionary, announced brightly, "A hobo is a person who has no permanent home and who moves from place to place."

"If you ask me, they are a disgrace," added Sophie.

"I'm glad the police told the hobos to leave town," said Lee.

"But this man was taking care of a dog. He seemed….." Terry tried to speak again, but no one was paying attention to him.

LEMONA
5¢

A short time later, Charlie came walking up the street.
He saw several children gathered around a lemonade
stand, and one of their mothers was there holding a jug
of lemonade. How wonderful it would be to sip a glass
of cold lemonade, he thought; something sweet and
cool to wash the dust out of his throat.

When he was in front of the stand Charlie bowed. "A good afternoon to you. My name is Charlie and I would love to have a glass of that lemonade. I have no money, but I would gladly pay for a glass by doing some work."

"My dad says that hobos are freeloaders who move from place to place," Max said.

Jenny wrinkled her nose, and whispered in her friend Sophie's ear. "I bet he smells bad," she said. The two girls then laughed behind their cupped hands, their eyes sparkling with sharp thoughts.

"Children, that is quite enough," said Sophie's mother. "Many people have lost their jobs and are doing the best they can. These are hard times."

LEMONADE
5¢

17

Charlie looked at the children with sad eyes. He had heard this kind of thing many times before. "It is true that hobos move from place to place," he said. "But it is not true that we are freeloaders. Likewise, we are not tramps or bums. Most of us are happy to work for food. We don't expect to get something for nothing."

"You should get a job," Lee said looking at Charlie.

"I use to have a job working in a bank, but the bank closed. I tried to find another job, but there were none to be had," Charlie explained.

Lee was reminded of his Uncle Jack. Uncle Jack had lost his job too, and now he had to live with his sister, Aunt Emily, because he didn't have any money. Lee looked at Charlie, and the sad look in the man's eyes was familiar. It was the same look that Uncle Jack had in his eyes.

"I may not be able to work in a bank any more, but I can do something else," Charlie said with a twinkle in his eyes. He took some stones out of his pockets and began to juggle them. Higher and higher the stones went. Quite forgetting about his dusty clothes and grimy face, the children gathered around Charlie, squealing with delight and clapping their hands.

Then Charlie tripped on a stone and he lost his balance. Down came the stones, and down went Charlie. The hobo laughed as he sat in the path. The children all reached out, and with pulls and tugs, they got Charlie back on to his feet. As he stood up, a chalk stick fell out of his pocket.

"Is that a chalk stick?" Jenny asked.

"Indeed it is," Charlie replied, bending down to pick it up. "We hobos use chalk symbols to leave messages for each other," Charlie said. "Here, let me show you."

Carefully, Charlie bent down and drew two pictures on the sidewalk. "If a hobo draws a picture of three diagonal lines like this, it means that the place is not safe. Can anyone guess what this sign means?" he asked as he drew a figure resembling a spider.

"Spider legs," Jenny said giggling.

"I will remember that," Charlie said with a chuckle. "What it means in hobo language is that there is a dog nearby who isn't friendly. If I see that sign I know that I have to get ready to run away as fast as I can."

All the children laughed when they heard these words.

"You know, as I was making my way toward your lemonade stand, I spotted a few chalk symbols right here in your neighborhood," Charlie declared.

"Can you show them to us?" Sophie asked all of a sudden.

"I'd like to see them too," Sophie's mother said smiling.

"I have my magnifying glass all ready," added Terry.

23

The group started to walk down the street.

"See here," Charlie said pointing to where the letters T and an X inside a circle had been chalked on a gate post. "The T means that people here will give you food if you work for them, and an X inside a circle means that the people will give you food if you ask for it."

"That's my house!" exclaimed Lee in surprise.

"And see that little drawing of a cat on that tree over there?" said Charlie. "That sign means that a kindhearted lady lives in the house nearby."

"That tree is in front of my grandma's house," Jenny said with pride.

All the children knew Jenny's grandma was a very nice lady.

Just then, the children noticed that a little dog was following them. "Whose dog is that?" Max asked.

"Well, I guess he is mine," Charlie answered with a smile. "We found each other in the hobo village earlier today."

"And you took care of him by fixing his sore leg. He also needed water and food, and you gave him those things too. I saw you," Terry said with pride.

Charlie smiled at Terry. "He needed help, didn't he?"

The other children looked from Terry to Charlie. Sophie lowered her head. She had said this man was a disgrace, but he wasn't. He wasn't a disgrace at all.

"Mr. Charlie, would you like some lemonade?" Sophie asked.

"A glass of lemonade is just what I need before I hop on the five o'clock train," he replied.

Sophie led everyone back to the lemonade stand. Carefully, she poured out a big glass of lemonade and handed it to Charlie.

"Thank you kindly," Charlie said with a grateful smile.

While Charlie sipped the lemonade, Sophie's mother quickly disappeared inside her house. Soon she came back and stood before Charlie.

"Here," she said handing a paper sack to Charlie. "I have put some food in this bag to keep you going until you can get some work further along the rail line. I included some treats for your dog too," she added with a smile.

"Much obliged," Charlie said tipping his hat to Sophie's mother.

A train whistle blew in the distance. "It's time for me to leave," the hobo said. The children were all sorry to see their new friend go.

"Let's all walk Charlie and this little tail-wagger to the railroad tracks," said Sophie's mother glancing toward the dog.

Before he climbed into a boxcar, Charlie shook hands with each of the children, and as the train pulled away, the children waved their hands eagerly at the man and his dog.

"I'll visit you all the next time I'm back this way," Charlie shouted out. Then he waved his hat good-bye as the train, with the clickety-clack of its steel wheels, disappeared around a corner and was gone.

"Come on Terry, you can help take care of the lemonade stand when we get back. I'll race you," Sophie said, and the children all took off running.

When they got back to the lemonade stand, the children saw that Charlie had drawn another symbol on the sidewalk before he had left. None of the children needed Charlie to tell them what it meant.

# HOBO SIGNS

AFRAID

CAMP HERE

DOCTOR HERE

DOG

DON'T GIVE UP

GO

HANDOUT HERE

CATCH A TRAIN

FOLLOW ROAD

IN

KEEP QUIET

KIND WOMAN

MAN

OUT

NOT SAFE

POLICE

RICH

SIT DOWN

STOP

TELEPHONE

TELL A SAD STORY

GOOD

WILL CARE FOR YOU IF SICK

WOMAN

WORK FOR FOOD HERE

# Glossary

Bindle - a term used to describe the bag, sack, or carrying device used by the sub-culture of hobos.

Bindle Stick - a stick to which the "bindle" was affixed, and is carried across the shoulder.

Boxcar - a fully enclosed railroad car on a train, with a sliding door used to transport freight.

Bum - a homeless person who does not work, and who begs for a living in one place.

Bundle - a number of things wrapped or tied up for carrying.

Dick Tracy - a tough and intelligent police detective using question and answer methods and advanced gadgetry to become a hero crime fighter in an American comic strip from 1931 -1977.

Freeloader - a person who is always accepting free food and a place to stay without giving them anything in return.

Great Depression - a period when there was a worldwide economic depression and unemployment lasting until the late 1930s or middle 1940s.

Handkerchief - a square of cloth with unlimited uses.

Hobo - a homeless person who travels from place to place looking for work, often by "freight hopping" (illegally catching rides on freight trains.)

Hobo Village - a collection of huts and shacks also known as a Hooverville at the edge of a city, housing the unemployed during the 1930s. People who lost their homes blamed their conditions on President Hoover when the Great Depression began.

Mulligan Stew - a stew made of bits of various meats and vegetables.

Symbols - a sign, number, letter, etc. that has a fixed meaning.

Tramp - a person who does not seek regular work and supports themselves by other means such as begging or scavenging.

# Historical Note

The stock-market crash of October 29, 1929, affected the nation for well over a decade. Tens of thousands of companies failed, and banks closed their doors, taking people's life savings with them. Crop prices dropped, causing many farmers to loose their farms and their livelihood. Many people became unemployed because of the crash, and people began to call that time in history the Great Depression.

By the 1930s, railway tracks crisscrossed the country, and trains were running to every bustling market town in America. When the Great Depression began, the unemployed began to use freight trains to travel around the country. Hopping on the trains illegally, they went looking for work and for a better life. They became hobos, and finding food was a huge problem as they made their way across the country looking for jobs.

To cope with the problems associated with the hobo way of life, hobos developed a system of signs and symbols. They used chalk or coal images to tell each other where to find work, where a meal could be had, directions to places, and to warn one another of danger. Town residents often considered hobos to be lazy transients, but there were some people who understood that they were victims of the hard times.

No one is quite sure where the term hobo came from. It has been suggested that it originated in the Western United States where the term hoe-boy, meaning farmhand, is used. It may perhaps be a contraction of the phrase <u>ho</u>meward <u>bo</u>und, or have its roots in the railroad greeting, <u>ho</u> <u>beau</u>. Still others reason that the name stems from the junction of <u>Ho</u>uston and the <u>Bo</u>wery in Manhattan, where rovers once gathered. The city of <u>Hobo</u>ken in New Jersey, a last stop for many railroad lines in the nineteenth century, may also be the source of the name. Since many hobos moved from place to place by <u>ho</u>pping <u>bo</u>xcars, the name may perhaps have its source in their chosen form of transportation. Whatever its history might be, the word hobo refers to a person who is a traveling worker.

# About the Author

Minnesota author, Renée Wendinger, is a history essayist who writes for a wide demographic spectrum of readers of all ages. She has received numerous awards for her work, including two time history winner of the NIEA Excellence in book awards for her published nonfiction, *Extra! Extra! The Orphan Trains and Newsboys of New York* and her historical novella, *Last Train Home: An Orphan Train Story.*

*Charlie's Chalk Stick* is Renée's original children's story filled with fresh, interesting, and well researched history in support of discovery learning.

# About the Illustrator

Sharon Grey has worked as a children's book illustrator for six years. She received training in art from Black Hills State and Baylor Universities, and now devotes her time to drawing and painting. In art, her favorite subject matter is children. In real life, her favorite subject matter is also children, specifically her three children, Cordelia, Charlotte and Ethan.

Sharon lives in the Black Hills of South Dakota with her husband, daughters, dogs and cats. *Charlie's Chalk Stick* is her twentieth illustrated book, and Sharon looks forward to working on many more.